BP
32

AF669449

THE BOTTOM LINE

by

SONU V C

World Book Company (P) Limited.

2012 Copyright © Sonu V C
First printed in September 2012 All rights reserved
ISBN – 978-93-82417-19-4
Price: ₹199/-

Author asserts his/her moral right to be identified as the author of this book'.
This book may not be reproduced in whole or in part, in any form or by any means, electronic, mechanical, photocopying, recording, or by any information storage and retrieval system now known or hereafter invented, without prior written permission from the publisher, except for reading and browsing via the World Wide Web and that is also through authorised sale to intended person only.

Cover Design by Bikram Sarkar
Book layout by ABC PREMEDIA, a division of World Book Company

Edited by Sunita Kapri

Published by World Book Company

World Book Company (P) Limited
Regd. Office: B-911, DDA MIG Flats, Chitrakoot, New Delhi-110093.
Corporate Office: F-11, 2F, Mahaluxmi Metro Tower, Opp. Vaishali Metro Station, Vaishali-201011, New Delhi NCR.

Lord Almighty Bless Us

Dedicated to my beloved wife Dimpy...Just want to tell her "I love you"

Foreword

I would like to begin by congratulating Sonu for 'The Bottom Line', which I hope will be the first of many of his penmanships.

Leafing through the book, I can only ascertain that the bug has bitten him. The bug that no doubt has left mankind befuddled, over and over again. Questions like 'Why are we here?' and 'Is there a purpose beyond our everyday existence?' seem to have tickled and consumed the mind of my young and very talented ex-colleague.

This book may not give you all the answers. Perhaps no single book can. But it does leave you with enough food for thought and musing. It does set you into a reflective pause; perhaps precisely what the author wanted to achieve.

I wish him all the best.

Warmly,

Harshavardhan Neotia

Chairman

Ambuja Neotia

Acknowledgements

- Let me at first thank the Almighty for giving me the wisdom and understanding to write such a deep subject
- Let me thank my mother Ms. Aleyamma N K to be a part of my life
- Heartfelt thanks to all my relatives and family members to be a part of my life
- Sincere thanks to all my teachers, mentors, friends and colleagues, especially to:

Mentors/Teachers: Late Prof. Rajat Dutta, Mr. Surendra Rajpurohit, Mr. Kapil Pandla, Ms. Jaya, Ms. Bindu Nair, Ms. Ananta Bhardwaj, Prof. J M Pant, Mr. Lokesh Sinha, Mr. Kishore Singh, Ms. Ritu Verma, Ms.Amutha, Mr. Harshavardhan Neotia, Mr. Kan Singh Sodha, Mr. V S Dwivedi, Mr. P Sandeep

Friends/Colleagues: Mr. Anand Bhandari, Mr. Gaurav Shukla, Mr. Karamveer Rajguru, Mr. Gaurav Khatri, Mr. Vinod Kumar Jain, Ms. Medha Sharma, Ms. Nupur Goyal, Mr. K M Pillai, Mr. Sailesh Jaiswal, Mr. Sanjay B Gaikwad, Mr. AS Sreenadh, Mr. Suvadeep Mullick, Mr. Yusuf Khan, Mr. Devanshu Verma, Ms. Aniji Varghese, Mr. Bikram Sarkar.

Author's Note

Let me clearly inform all the readers that this book is not a magic stick or an angel that will provide you the answers to all your questions pertaining to birth and life (existence).

Understanding life has never been that easy. Life unfolds new and different colours now and then. People spend years to understand life and I am no one to comment that I have understood even a percent of it. Although it is not that complex but it is not that simple too.

The purpose of writing this book is to provide few threads (ideas), based on my exposure, experience, introspection and knowing a little bit here and there, to all of you. And I strongly believe that these ideas can act as enablers in identifying your purpose of life. It does not talk about anything which is unheard or unseen of. The sole purpose is to give you a pause and take you a step back from your current state so that you can visualise the broader perspectives of life and think about the very purpose of your existence.

Each individual is different and each one of us has got different aims and goals in life. This book tells that: yes, although we may have different aims and goals, yet the bottom line i.e. the end remains the same for each one of us. However, to achieve the bottom line we need to define the means to reach the end. The means may vary from individual to individual depending on a lot of factors.

The irony is that most of us have actually defined and concluded the means as the purpose of our life. We always work towards achieving those, throughout our lives and at some point of time (usually during old age), we realise something is missing and that 'something' is nothing but 'the bottom line'.

The book intends to help you understand the bottom line i.e. the end, by clarifying the distinction between the means and the end. Hope by the time you complete reading this book and comprehend it, you will be able to differentiate between the means and the end i.e. the true purpose of life, so that you can define your road map and then put all your efforts and energy to achieve the final destination i.e. the end.

How close do you reach the final destination and how correctly you define your means to reach there, totally depends on you because I strongly believe that it is YOU and only YOU who can make a difference to your life and no one else.

Let me pray and hope that this book will act as a guide, a mentor and a friend to your life.

Sonu V C

Contents

Why Birth?

Since quite long, few questions about the true meaning and the purpose of birth have been bothering me a lot. – 'Who am I?' What am I born for? Does my birth have any specific purpose? Why this life at all? And many more questions related to my existence. At some point in life, people generally ask these questions to themselves and I am no exception. Some think over it for few days, some for few months and some for few years, depending on how much the topic interests them. There are only few who are actually interested in discovering the answer to these questions and most likely this is because they truly yearn for. For others, it is just a thought, like any other one, at that particular point of time and the next moment they get busy with their usual lives.

When people start pondering over these questions,

in the management terminology, they are usually being labelled to be on the self-actualisation stage. This is the phase when human beings want to know about their true existence and they do put in effort towards getting the answer for the same. But is it not unfortunate that this journey of self actualisation in most of our lives start when we are almost at the end of our career or life i.e. the retirement age! And if by mistake, someone starts pondering over these questions at a young age, he would either be labelled as over-smart or boring, by the people around him. Are we to be blamed for it or do we look for someone else, so that we can pass on the buck to others? Given an option, we would tend to do the latter. But the question is still there; why all these? Are we so engrossed with our day to day routine lives that we do not even have time to find the answer for our mere existence?

But then again, a question arises in my mind that we do take out time for movies, for vacations, for shopping, for rejuvenation, and of course for parties, and if we can take out time for all these materialistic things then how can we neglect or ignore thinking about the very purpose of our life?

Understanding life has always been the most difficult thing and it is not at all a cake walk. Life reveals its different colours every moment. Neither yesterday nor tomorrow will be the same as today. What worked in a particular situation does not seem to fit the other? What is true in one's case may not be the same in other's case? What seems beautiful to one may not be the same for someone else? We, human beings have our own limitations but we try and put our experience and exposure of life to comprehend its practical part up to a certain level. Surely, no one except the Lord Almighty, the creator, can claim that he understands the life wholely.

Let me go back to my school days when I used to love reading inspirational quotes and one of the lines from Swami Vivekananda's lectures, on the back cover of a notebook, actually triggered my mind to find the real and true purpose of life. He said *"Get up, and set your shoulder to the wheel - How long is this life for? As you have come into this world, leave some mark behind. Otherwise, where is the difference between you and the trees and stones? They too come into existence, decay and die."*

What mark can we leave behind? How can we be different from trees and stones? How can we actually give meaning to our lives? Has our life got any meaning at all? My mind was bombarded with a lot of questions at one go.

I thought for a while and then I asked myself, "Does it mean I will have to lead my life like a *Monk,* a *Father* or as a *Sadhu*? Does it mean I need to do away with the practical/materialistic world? Does it mean I will have to abandon my family? Does it mean I will never get married and will never have children?" My mind was blistering with questions. I relaxed my brain for a few seconds and then suddenly I realised that I am on a very tricky track and it would be wise enough for me to discontinue these thoughts then and there. I did what my mind said. I do not know whether it was truly a wise decision or not but I was swayed away by my mind and I followed, what it said.

Days passed by and I got busy with the routine life. I completed my studies and like any other individual, I was also looking forward for a job. By the end of my management studies, I got an offer to work with a corporate house. I knew it was the beginning of my professional life. I thought of doing something great in my career. I worked hard for it. My efforts, passion and prayers paid off, I grew in my organisation better than others and I was quite happy about it. However, there was something which I was not very much contented about but I didn't want to stress myself by getting to be acquainted with what it was, so I left it there.

Heart of my heart I had this feeling that 'May be I am doing well on my career front, but is this, what I want to do in life? Do I want to be the HR Head? Do I want to be the Business Head? What do I want to be?' However, what bothered me the most was – 'why do I want to be whatever I want to be? I had no answers to all these.' When I joined my management studies, I was like most of my batch associates, who did not know for what were we pursuing our management studies and how was it going to impact our and others lives. I do not know whether by this time we are matured enough to think about our lives or not, but that time certainly we were in darkness and our decisions were guided by unimportant factors like friend's interest to do management studies, people's view that management job pays well, so on and so forth. Forget about the ultimate goal, we were not even clear about our short term goals. Shockingly, this is true with a lot of people.

I recollected my thoughts of those good old days

when I got inspired by that particular quote by Swami Vivekananda and I said to myself, "It's high time that I should find answers to all those questions."

I realised that I was back to square one, with the same questions in my mind but this time with a greater energy, impact and enthusiasm that it was in fact difficult for me to do away with it. I read few books on life, searched about the meaning and purpose of life on internet and interacted with learned people seeking an answer for the true meaning of life. It helped me; of course it helped me but not to get the answers. It essentially set the track right by encouraging me that what I was thinking was nothing unusual. People do think about it at some point in life and I was lucky that I was onto it at the age of twenty five. But believe me even then I didn't want to be a *Sadhu*, a *Monk* or a *Father*, not that it was something bad but because it certainly was not my cup of tea. It actually takes a lot to lead such a life and I indeed didn't know whether I can at all do it or not.

I have a habit of talking to myself, intellectuals call it *Introspection*. Yes, I usually used to do it even then. I thought why not introspect on these questions and the lives of few people. The idea was interesting for me and moreover because I loved introspecting I said "Let me do this."

The process started and I was flooded with questions from within. This continued for few months and the hazy picture started getting clearer. I knew at least I was on the right track. My efforts were paying off and I was feeling as if I was growing from within.

The creator, the Lord Almighty, had made the difference between us and the trees and stones when he created this world by putting us above all other creatures and things. Lot of people say probably human being is the most beautiful and unique creation of God. We human beings have also been gifted, by the Almighty, the beautiful and creative brain which can think, memorise and interpret and what not. Human beings have done wonders through their brain. We have achieved things which were beyond imaginations. Great innovations, researches, discoveries, inventions etc. have taken place and it is no one other than the human beings who have done it. We are certainly different from trees and stones but now the question is how? Is it the appearance or the brain that differentiates us from them? Whether it is the brain or the appearance, both the differences were created at the beginning of this creation by the Lord Almighty, so then, how have we contributed in being different? How have we done things differently that could differentiate us from them? How have we done justice to the brain and the appearance that differentiates us?

To understand this very basic purpose is important but to get a solution to any problem or question, it is quite important to collect the facts which are given or are available. Similarly in solving this question it is important to understand the human life i.e. the practical life that each one of us is leading. Generations over generations have led their practical life in a particular fashion, of course with time; things have changed with the basics unchanged.

When analysed deeply, I understood almost 99.9 per cent of the population spend their practical lives in the following manner:

Birth - Education - Job - Marriage - Children - Children's Education - Children's Job - Children's Marriage - Retirement from job - Grand Children and the cycle continues hereafter in the similar fashion until death

Science has advanced a lot over the years. We have answers for how a baby is born but how the life ends is still a question mark. Why death and what after death, is something science is still looking forward to get an answer on. What happens before birth and what happens after death is not known to me? I haven't seen or experienced it. So I decided not to indulge myself in the pre-birth and post-death episode. I said "Let the competent people think over it; research over it."

Although I have read and also heard from quite a numbers of people on death and life afterwards, some believe that after death there is rebirth but not as human beings again, for others there is still life even after death and many related things. This was something which was beyond my reach and I didn't want to make an imaginary comment on it. So I left it there and focused on what happens between the period of birth and death i.e. the life that an individual spends on earth.

But then again, is this the way life has to be led? Is the purpose to get educated, then a decent job, handsome salary package, a respectable designation, then get married, have children, their education and marriage and then finally death one day? What about the purpose of life? I certainly couldn't believe that I was born to do only this. I was definitely not convinced but could not also ignore that this is how we all lead our life.

That was the day I realised that this is the practical way of leading the life with two ends fixed, one '*the birth*' and other one '*the death*'. These two events are bound to happen, without fail.

This is how most of us spend our lives and we can't ignore this part of our life. Yes, the degree of how the life is led may vary depending on whether you were born in a rich family or in a financially poor family, whether you were born physically challenged or not, whether you earn handsome salary package or not, whether your parents have crores to spend on your marriage or not and many more factors into it. The degree is important because it defines how well and how smoothly you lead your life. However, it is also important to note that rich or poor; educated or uneducated; men or women; each one of us go through both the rough and the smooth patches in life. No one is excused just because he or she is rich and powerful. Luckily, the judgement here is not by any human being, who is always surrounded by hunger for materialistic possessions, pressure, fear and what not. The unbiased decision comes from the Lord Almighty.

In quest of exploring more on this front, I started interacting with people whom I have known and was in contact, specially my colleagues and friends. I asked them what do they want to be in their lives and the responses that I got were:

- I want to become the CEO of a multinational company.
- I want to earn a lot of money.
- I do not know!
- I want to become the HR Head of a reputed company.
- I want to be a Business Tycoon.
- I want to own a firm.
- I want to start my consulting business.
- I want to be a Doctor.
- I want to become an Engineer.
- I am confused!

- I want to be get into modelling.
- I want to join Indian Administrative Services.
- I want to join Indian Army and what not?

Different people have different views, goals and aims, and it has to be. Individuals set their aims and goals depending on what interests them and there is absolutely nothing wrong with it. My perception that most of the people are not focused put me in a false position, after this exercise. Although there were people who were confused as to what they want to be in their lives but most of them had an idea of what they were running after. Some knew what to achieve in life but did not know why to achieve whatever they have planned. Some did not even know what to achieve, the most confused lot. Which one is a tragedy; knowing what to achieve but not knowing why or not even knowing what to achieve? Certainly both. May be the latter one is the bigger tragedy but not knowing why you want to achieve whatever you have aimed at is also not at all a very happy state.

Shockingly! when I asked them as to why they want to achieve all these, the responses I got were, they either wanted to buy a nice house for them, a nice car, a nice bungalow or to achieve a status in the society or wanted to enjoy the luxuries available. But what will these materialistic possessions get us? What will we do with them when we will leave from this world? Can wealth defy death? For whom are we creating this wealth? Is it for our children? Do we know who is going to die first, they or we? Have we not seen people who have lost their beloved ones for whom they were creating all wealth?

After lot of introspection, I realised life is much more than just the practical life. We made this world how it is and we are following the same. What will money get us? What will the professional growth get us? Is this all about chasing after the wind? Is this all vanity? If yes, should we do away with it? Should we not earn? Should we not fulfil our dreams of becoming the CEO or something that we have dreamt and desired for?

There is much left to understand but one thing is final i.e. there are two lines that guides our lives, one the practical line and the other one the bottom line. Practical line answers 'what' and bottom line answers 'why and how'. They are interlinked to each other, the way the means is to the end.

Avatar or Angel

Avatar, generally is defined as an incarnation, appearance or form. Can the lives of Lord Jesus, Lord Rama, Lord Krishna, Lord Buddha and Lord Mahaveer be referred as avatars? May or may not be. Different people may have different views on it but let us understand that it is no debate. What is important is, to understand their lives so that we can draw inferences to get answers for our mere existence. We might have not seen them but we have heard of their human incarnation. They too lived like us, the practical way. What then is the difference between them and us? Is it that they were God in human incarnation and we are just human beings? May be it is true because we do not know, where do we come from? Science can throw some light on it by means of their scientific discoveries and logics but what about our purpose of life? They probably will not be able to answer;

why this life at all?

Lord Jesus, Lord Rama, Lord Krishna, Lord Buddha and Lord Mahaveer led their practical lives as we do. How then are we so different from them? They all might have lived their lives in different ways but their bottom line was always the same. Did anyone of them live for themselves? Did they try and create wealth for themselves? Did they think of their share before others benefit? Were they not the reflection of God? These questions are for us to ponder on, but what is more important to think is about our lives so that we can relate it with that of theirs.

Is birth, an Avatar (Incarnation) or are we Angels? The questions are tricky. May be neither of these questions fit the bill or both of them.

We too have taken birth as human beings. I am not aware, whether we are incarnation or not, in true form? Whether we are avatars, in true form or not? Can we treat our lives as avatars and feel that we are angels? Will it be an imagination? Not very sure! May be for few of us certainly it is because we have never seen real angels in our lives, nor have we got an opportunity to meet them.

I cannot stop thinking about my childhood days when I used to dream of angels who can fulfil my little wishes and bring happiness in my life. I used to spend hours in hope of them. With passage of time I got busy with my routine life but believe me even today, I feel the need of an angel.

Are there real angels ? Do they really exist? Will they fulfil my dreams? These are the questions which keep on bothering me. Truly speaking, I have no clue about their existence. The story books talk about them and we, all through our childhood get fascinated by stories and think of them. Maturity brings in a lot of positives but some negatives too. We stop imagining about angels now; probably we cannot because we are being tagged as matured.

We may take the shade of maturity to forget about angels but believe me life brings all in place and with time we realise the need of them, mostly during our hard or tough times. We cannot do away with it.

I am sure; I am not the only one who wants to have angels in my life. There are many more like me. Children or adult, educated or uneducated, poor or rich, men or women, student or teacher, patient or doctor everyone desires to have angels in their lives. Certainly, the need for the same increases when one is in trouble, other than children who keep their hopes on angels and the fairy tales all the times. They feel that some angel from nowhere will come and fulfil their dreams of getting a bicycle, toy, chocolates, computer, teddy bear and what not. Does it actually happen? Do their wishes get fulfilled or with time they also understand that it just happens in stories?

The fact remains that at any given point of time, someone, somewhere is going through this phase of life and is expecting an angel in his/her life, just like us. There are children who just wish for someone who could take care of their education; who could provide them a proper meal for a day. There are people, who are unable to survive just because of poor financial conditions; who cannot afford to buy medicines for their loved ones just because they do not earn enough. They all expect some wonders through angels in their lives. They look forward for some helping hands.

This reminds me about one of the incidents which took place just few months back when I was in Kolkata. One of my colleagues' wife was suffering from some severe pain in stomach for quite a few days. Her husband took her to a nearby clinic for check-up. The doctor expected it may be a stone problem and advised for some medical tests before confirming the same. He was stressed because of his financial condition. Somehow, he managed some money from here and there and got the tests done. He was now eagerly waiting for the reports and was praying to the Lord Almighty that let this be a normal pain instead of stone. After examining all the necessary medical test reports, the doctors confirmed that his wife was actually a cancer patient and needed to be operated. As soon as the news broke, he lost all his hopes. Not because he didn't want to get his wife operated or didn't love his wife but because he knew his financial condition will not permit him to get his wife operated. Like any other loving husband, he too loved his wife very much but he seemed helpless. For someone who was not even hopeful of managing the amount for a stone operation, it was nearly impossible for him to arrange money for cancer operation? He completely broke down. I am sure he was looking for an angel in his life. He was actually looking for the financial help, the helping hands. This is one such case but I am sure similar incidents happen with a lot of people and they just look forward for some kind of help. Do we have any role to play? Can we be of any help to them? Can we actually act as angels for them?

For a moment, just think:

Had there been a moment in your life when you were completely frustrated or depressed and needed someone and you found one?

Had there been an incident, when you needed financial help and someone from nowhere came and helped you?

Had there been a moment when you were looking for a particular special gift on your birthday and you were not hopeful of getting it but surprisingly, someone got it for you?

Had there been a moment when you felt lonely and someone from nowhere came and cared for you? The examples can go on and on.

Somewhere, someday, something like these might have happened in our lives and will continue to happen. Many a times, it happens in life that we get help from people, we never expected or even we have never known before.

It happens but actually how many of us do try and understand who the chap was and why did he do so? Were his /her acts like an angel? Can we also act as angels to someone's life and make a difference? Are angels no one other than the human beings themselves? Difficult to comment but yes, human beings in some form act as angels, the practical life angels.

They can help, they can protect, they can guide the way any angel would do. But the sad part is that we do not even realise how important are we to someone's life. We do not understand how we can bring difference to someone's life. We do not know how we can bring happiness in someone's life. We are so busy with our own personal lives, desires and troubles that we do not even get time to think for others. But angels do not think for themselves, they live for others. Angels know what their purpose is? What they have been created for? They are unlike human beings, who are unaware of the purpose and meaning of life. But if we can make difference to anyone's life, we can act as angels to them and an angel in human form is nothing but Avatar.

Practical Line

Recently, a couple working in a multinational company got a few days off from their office. Excited about the holidays at hand, they planned to make it memorable by spending time at a beautiful place. What a beautiful and commendable thought! Isn't it?

Preparations started and the first thing they planned to decide was the place. With planning, problems started cropping in. Their views on different matters started differing, not just on finalising the place of visit but the mode of transport and the hotel also. The beautiful thought started turning into a nightmare. He was not happy with something; on the other side she was also not pleased with some other things. Finally, after so many ifs and buts they finalised their tour and kicked off for spending their holidays to make them memorable. No doubt, that the tour kicked off, but will it happen the way they have planned it? Are they still excited about the holidays, the way they were before? Will they enjoy the holidays or just accuse each other for something or the other? The story may differ from case to case, but what happened in this case was not very pleasing. Although, they managed to keep their promise of going out for a tour but they could not manage their happiness and returned after the holidays with a very dissatisfying experience.

What! Oh no!

Is it not surprising?

The ones, who have planned for the tour themselves, are not happy now. But why? What exactly went wrong? Do not they love each other? If yes they do, then why was their beautiful thought of a memorable trip got spoiled? Why wasn't their dream of spending quality time with each other fulfilled? Analyse or get to the root cause and one will realise that it was nothing but their focus getting shifted from the end to the means. While deciding on the means i.e. the place of visit, the mode of transport etc. they forgot the sole purpose of the visit. They forgot that it was actually to spend quality time with each other and make it memorable.

What happened with this couple was not very unusual, it happens with most of us many a times. Although, the scenarios may differ and the results may also vary but to what extent, only time can unveil. Generally, by the time we decide on the means, we have already screwed up our end. The means, in the process, become so important and crucial that we are ready to even compromise with the end without realising the consequences of it.

Can a trainer deliver an efficient and effective training without knowing what should be the outcome? Can an HR professional achieve the deliverables without knowing the mere existence of HR function? Can an author write a book without knowing what is expected out of it? Can a doctor operate a patient without knowing what to operate for? If the answer in most of the cases is 'No', then how can we compromise with the end? The end is certainly above all as it is the mere purpose of doing whatever we are planning to do, and therefore it becomes very important and unavoidable.

Once we finalise the end, means are to be decided to help us to achieve whatever we have planned for and take us to the final destination. Can they become so important in the process that we start ignoring the end and settle down with the means?

Systems and processes have been 'the buzz words' in the corporate world and other institutions as well for quite long. We do need systems and processes at different stages and levels to streamline various functions, roles etc. But just imagine, what would happen if in the process of creating systems and processes, to attain certain objectives, the systems and processes in itself become so important and inevitable that we forget the mere purpose of creating it. Will this be a healthy situation? If not, then can we do away with the systems and processes? Is it possible to reach the end without the means? The next few pages should unfold the answers to these questions.

If we consider 60 as the average age of human life, we spend nearly half the age in getting educated and looking for a decent job. The remaining of the practical life is spent in getting married, having children, their education and marriage and along these lines we are constantly striving to get a handsome bank balance, a nice house, a nice car, a respectable designation, so on and so forth. By the time we realise, it is actually the time for us to say adieu to this world. What happens then is not known to any one of us. But certainly, the house, the bank balance, the designation and the car everything is taken away from you and you are asked to return to your original place the way you had entered the practical life, empty handed.

If this is what happens finally, then why all these?

Why have desires to get educated, get a job, get married, have children, earn handsome salary or money so on and so forth? Is this all chasing after the wind or all these essential to survive in the so called "life" or some social obligations or are all these means to achieve the end?

Imagine the lives of the people who are not well educated, who do not have a decent job, who do not have a handsome salary and a huge bank balance. Do people recognise them? Probably, to even survive in this world is itself a challenge for them. Then what, should we go for it or not? Hope I have not put you in a dilemma.

If you are in the computer age and you do not know

how to operate computers, it is quite possible that people may call you uneducated. Although it may not be the truth but life, the practical life, is like that. If you say, I do not need money to survive; people may call you a fool because as per the practical life you cannot purchase anything if you do not have money.

The world around us i.e. the practical life that we operate in, has got certain defined norms and rules. Can we go to a market place and purchase a laptop for our self or even a toy for our children without money? Can we apply for certain written examinations without qualifying the requirements or for certain jobs without the required qualification and percentage of marks? Can we vote or apply for driving licence before attaining a certain age? 'The Cans' can go on and on. The point is who made all these rules and norms. Is it being created by the creator or are these being created by the human being itself? Undoubtedly, we have created a practical life around us and now we live according to it. We brought all these concepts and today we are just following them.

Good or bad, this is how it has been devised. Who knows with the time to come, things may change or remain the same? Earlier it was the barter system, people used to give 2 kg of sugar to get 3 kg of wheat. Today the scenario has changed a lot and money has become the mother of all transactions. Probably, new systems may come in and then we will start following those. Who knows? Let us not talk about something which is uncertain, the future.

Take a holistic view to try and understand the practical life, one will realise that it recognises the importance of two most important things – Health and Wealth. These define the rules of the game. The latter certainly has a greater impact on the human beings and we tend to do or link almost all our activities to create more of it for us and our family members. God knows for what? Just take a moment to think, are we born to create wealth or to be healthy? Is this the way, we are going to impact the world and make a mark? What if tomorrow or right at this moment, death knocks our door? Are we not actually chasing after the wind?

There is no doubt that health and wealth are important. No one of us can discount this very fact as this is the reality of the practical life and being a part of it, we can, in no ways, do away with it.

But are these not only the means to achieve the final destination decided by us or are we born just to be healthy and wealthy? Sad to say but this is what almost everyone in this world is after, running the rat race.

The same is true with professional achievement also. Why do we want to be the HR Head? Why a Business Head? Why an Actor? Why Cricketer? Were we born to do become any of these? Whether it is an HR Head, a Business Head, an Actor or a Cricketer, the practical world i.e. the people around, recognises the importance of professional achievement and therefore to make a mark one has to take this, first most important leap. Otherwise, no one is interested to know and to talk about you. You have to be a part of the system to change the system. Therefore, is this achievement not a means to the journey? Unfortunately, everyone is so lost in the illusion of the practical life that we start running the race for making name for ourselves without knowing why and it becomes the be all and end all. Is this the bottom line? Are we the part of this race to make name for ourselves? What do we want to achieve by this? Do we want people to remember our names? Do we want people to make a poster of ours and worship?

Holy cow, let us not take the place of the Almighty. What after professional achievement or why professional achievement, will give you the bottom line The professional achievement is just another milestone on the practical line.

You might be thinking what this practical line is? We have heard of practical life quite often but not a practical line. Let me tell you that this is no new concept or rocket science.

Practical line is nothing but the practical life which anyone of us would lead with the practical world in focus. Practical line helps in achieving the bottom line.

The tragedy is not that we are following the practical line, it is that we have defined our practical line as our bottom line i.e. the means have actually become the end for us. In the process of creating this practical world, we, human beings have actually forgotten that the practical life was just to reach the destination. It, in itself cannot be the destination.

The practical line, in true terms is nothing but the

means to the end but the irony of human life is that we get so engrossed with our routine life or means that we tend to make it as our end and forget the true purpose of life i.e. the end.

We are the ones to decide whether we want to *"live to eat"* or *"eat to live"*. The choice is only and only ours.

Bottom Line

What is in our control?

We, human beings, want to have control over what not but the question is, do we actually have control over everything or nothing? Before we try and know about the bottom line, it is important for us to know what is in our control.

Does a pregnant lady know when is she going to deliver her baby? Does a student who has recently appeared for an examination know that he is going to make it? Does a candidate who has given an interview in a multinational company know that he is going to be shortlisted? Do we know when will be the last day of our lives? Can a rich person control his wealth and assure himself and his family members that he will never become poor? Are we sure that our place will not be hit by Tsunami or earthquake? Can we assure that nothing will go wrong with us? If the answer in most of the cases is 'NO', then what control are we talking of. Are we then not chasing after the wind? What then is in our control? If nothing, then why do we want to control everything? Why do we all run after power to control?

Is it really not strange that we cannot control anything but we want to have control over everything? Unbelievably, it is true that we human beings have very less to control but we feel that we can control anything and everything. The very less that we can control is the only thing that we can control and if we can understand what we can control, we probably can control everything. But the irony of human life is that we try to control what is not in our control and forget to control what is actually in our control. In the process we waste our energy and effort in achieving and controlling what is not in our control and we do not even give time to understand what is actually in our control. We are just happy with what we know and we do not want to understand, why are we in a state of discomfort? That's the beauty of life and that is why we say life is simple but at the same time it is complex too.

Few days back, I met one of my friends who seemed to be a bit disappointed and dejected. Out of curiosity and concern, I asked him, "What is wrong with you. Is everything ok?" He replied, "Not exactly". And then he started narrating the entire story. He was not happy because his superior had not rated him "Good" in the appraisal reviews and his salary hike was also not matched up to his expectations. This is not a very unique problem, it is pretty common and for HR professionals every appraisal exercise is a challenge in itself.

Can you imagine how just a rating by his seniors had made him unhappy? What went wrong? Has he actually not performed well?

He believed that he has performed as per the set standards but probably his equation with his senior wasn't that cordial and that was the reason for such rating. God knows the truth. As the saying goes, 'there is his part of the story, her part of the story and the truth'. Although, there was no mechanism for me to know whether he actually might have performed well or not, but knowing him for so many years I can just say that he is a focused and committed person. But then what next? Can my views that he is a person with high potential change his rating? Can my assurance to him to not to worry and everything will be alright, give him any sympathy?

The approach mattered and I wanted him to come out of his current state of mind. I knew he had given his control to someone else, otherwise how is it possible that his seniors rating can influence his thought process. I asked him, whether can he force his senior to change his rating? He replied, "No".

He wasn't acting unusual; this is what we all do when our expectations are not met. We tend to get negative and drive our thought process towards an unhappy state. This is what we call- not being in our own control. Someone from nowhere just comes and changes the complete scenario of our lives. The one who was very happy few months back and was expecting a nice appraisal this year, is no more in that state. Who is to be blamed for his unhappiness, his senior or he himself? He blamed his senior and I also had the option to do the same. May be his senior was biased, maybe he wasn't.

Just imagine, if he would have thought that his rating was in his seniors control and what maximum he could have done, was to give his best efforts, his life would have been much simpler. The mistake that he did and generally we all do is that we allow others to judge us and we forget that no one knows us better than ourselves. We are our chief judge. Does it mean that we should not be bothered about others feedback? Does it mean we become arrogant? Does it mean that we should not keep expectations? Does it mean that we should be mum and should not share our views and opinions?

No certainly not, we all have the right to share our views and keep expectations but what we should not forget is that we cannot control how others will react to us, we can only have control over our approach (thought process), attitude and actions and these are the only few things that we can control, nothing else.

You may ask your friend to accompany you for a movie, your girlfriend to wear a white suit, your children to pursue their career for so an so, your friend for some financial help, or you may get a very nice gift for your spouse on his/her birthday to make her happy, so on and so forth. But what is important to note is that you do not know how they will react or respond to it. You can only do what is in your control but not beyond that.

Love and Forgiveness

Love, probably one of the most sacred words with a deep sense of meaning is hardly understood in its purest form. We, human beings are intelligent enough to change things as per our convenience and certainly love has also not been spared. We only love, when we want to. It has become conditional with certain terms and conditions. But is it the right way to do so? If we love, only when we feel like or only those whom we like, then is it not being selfish? If we say, love is just between a boyfriend and a girlfriend then are we not restricting its dimension and boundaries?

If it is difficult to confine boundaries of air and light, just envision- how much more difficult it is to set boundaries for love, a feeling, which is omnipresent and omnipotent. Love, unquestionably has no boundaries. It does not discriminate people based on caste, creed, religion, colour, customs, country, continent or whatsoever. That is the beauty of it. But is this what we see in our day to day lives? Probably, the answer could be just opposite of what it actually stands for. People because of the illusion of the practical life have even sacrificed love. Nothing stands tall and strong when the human desires for materialistic possessions supersedes all, not even love.

Sad to say but the desire to be wealthy and powerful have made us not just blind but also absent minded. We have completely forgotten the mere purpose of our existence. Are we really doing something great by scarifying love for something so cheap as wealth and power, something of which we are not sure whether it will continue to be with us or not? If not, then why do it? Why not understand the importance of love before it is too late to be rectified and corrected? Why do we want to wait for life long and understand this simple truth, the harder way? Are we not that intelligent enough to differentiate between what is good for us and what is not? Certainly we are, but human desires take a toll on what we call love and it gets shadowed.

Each day which we spend is the only mark sheet that we have to our credit. We are not sure of tomorrow and this is the one and the only truth that no one can defy. Therefore it becomes moreover important for us to answer and reflect how we have spent the day that got added to our lives. If this is the truth then do we want to spend our day in sharing love or spreading hatred? Are we then being born to hate and to create difference among ourselves?

Are we born to talk ill of others? What do we gain, nothing but a so called and untrue satisfaction. Is it therefore not important that each day we spent we express and spread love to the people around us? Certainly true, but love cannot exist in isolation. It is incomplete without its companion and soul mate – the forgiveness. They both go hand in hand.

Can we think of fire without heat, can we think of sea without waves, if not how can we think of love without forgiveness? *Forgiveness is to love – the way breath is to life; pro is to con; tail is to head; one side is to the other side: inseparable.*

Amazingly true, how beautifully the creator had thought through in creating one of its most important or probably the most imperative creature, the human being! No one can question the efforts put in. We are certainly an astounding blend of love and forgiveness. Although, it is quite unfortunate that most of us are never able to understand this blend and unknowingly we usually act reverse of it in our day to day lives.

A common human life is full of love, hope, care, affection, expectations and desires, then how can we think of a life without fights, disappointments, frustration, anger etc.? Ask this question to people around you and they will say, "Yes Absolutely True" but just try and get hold of their nerves by getting angry on them for some or the other reason and you will experience a completely different picture. None of us wants others to be angry or unhappy with us but we have all the right to be so with them. Is it a fair game? Is this what we call the blend of love and forgiveness? No wonder how far have we moved from the state of love and forgiveness i.e. greatness, that the creator infused within us.

Do we not see people who have been friends few minutes back and suddenly something happens and the friendship goes for a toss? Friends turn into foes within no time. Just imagine, have we been blessed with understanding and wisdom (brain) to dislike and have fights but we do so, do not we? Also, have we been bestowed with a heart (beauty) to hate or ill treat those who have done something wrong or bad to us but we do so, do not we?

The brain i.e. understanding and wisdom, is there to help us to be good to others at all the times by spreading love and the beauty i.e., heart has been made so pure and graceful to help us forgive those who have knowingly or unknowingly done bad to us. Sad to say, but in the race to win accolades for ourselves, we human beings have forgotten how this life has to be led. Many a times, even the shadow of ego restrains us from forgiving others.

It is certainly of prime importance for us to answer and figure out whether we have been born to live with our ego which will come to an end with our uncertain lives or to spread love with forgiveness.

Strong Value System

A tree's strength lies in its roots. The stronger the root, the greater is its strength to withstand any calamity or wind. If the tree does not hold onto its roots, the probability of its fall in adverse conditions is much higher. We, human beings, are no different in this case. The root in our case is nothing but the value system that we have imbibed from parents, teachers, friends and our surroundings. It is needless to mention how important the role of parents and teachers in creating a value system is. They are the ones who help build the foundation of the building and if the foundation is weak the probability of its collapse is too high. The stronger the value system, the greater is the strength that it provides us to withstand all the adversaries of life.

Each one of us is tested in our practical lives at different times through different circumstances.

Who tests us and why we are tested, is something which no one can answer except the Supreme – the creator? We can just imagine or put a wild guess to it. In the difficult times, we have both the options either to kneel down and give away the teachings or to hold onto our value system and face it. Unfortunately, the former seems to be a more lucrative offer to all of us as it is the easiest to do and it gets us materialistic satisfaction. The latter brings in a lot many problems and hurdles.

Look around and you will observe that the practical life gives us thousands of examples of how the value system is being screwed in the quest of achieving something called the worldly possessions. Do we not see people who compromise to get higher designations and salaries? Do we not see people who compromise to get a better job? Do we not see people who compromise to be in the good books of their bosses? Do we not see people who compromise to earn money through false means? Do we not see people who compromise with a feeling of love just for some worldly gains? Is this how we are making a difference to this world? Is this how we want to make a mark? Whom are we really bluffing? May be for a moment, we may feel satisfied that we have deceived and cheated someone but are we not actually cheating ourselves? Are we born to cheat and deceive? What are we going to gain out of these? Are these not only the so called worldly possessions? What will these get us? Do we ever think what are we compromising with by doing all these? Aren't we actually compromising with our true selves?

Is it not really funny that we spend money and half

our age to understand and imbibe this value system through education and rest of our life we slowly do away with it just to earn that same money? Surprisingly true! but most of us do the same. How can we be so bad at brain? We are playing a game where in both the innings the loss is ours. In the first innings we lose money to gain values and in the second innings we lose values to gain money. The human intelligence is certainly under scrutiny and question. How are we then different from those who are uneducated? They might be doing the same out of ignorance but what about us? So should it be a matter of proud for us that we do it even after getting educated? Should we be awarded for it? It is for us to decide.

It is easier said than done. It is almost like wearing a WHITE SHIRT and protecting it from all the dirt around. No one can deny that it is a difficult job but then rather than saving ourselves from the dirt if we become party to it, what are we up to.

Selfless Life

Nature gives us ample of examples to learn from it. Is it that we are ignorant to it or we would like to be ignorant? Either of them may be true, however both the scenarios are in no ways a healthy sign for the humankind. It just portrays that we are not keen to know what is expected out of us or even after knowing what is expected out of us, we have turned off our faces from the reality. We have blocked learning from the surroundings.

We, human beings, have always been good at giving excuses and reasons. We have been doing it from our early childhood, whether it is to justify why we were late for school or why we have scored fewer marks in a particular subject or class. And over the years we train ourselves to be masters of justifying circumstances with reasons. Given an opportunity, we may also justify why we are ignorant to the nature's learning. Therefore, when Swami Vivekananda says "Make a mark, otherwise what is the difference between the trees, stones and you, they too come into existence, die and decay", we may have reasons to justify how we are different from trees and stones. Probably, the need here is not to justify others but ourselves. Hope we would not play with ourselves at least.

Yes, we are certainly different from the trees but the truth is- unlike them we grow being selfish. Look at them, they grow and nurture themselves to give shade and fruits to the needy. They teach us the beautiful law of selfless life i.e. a life for others. Not even for once do they think of their own interest.

It is quite unfortunate that we, human beings, even with our ability to think are unable to match up to the greatness of the trees when it comes to lead a selfless life. Is this how we want ourselves to be differentiated from the trees? If yes, then why not prefer trees to human beings.

When we are the most beautiful creation of the Lord Almighty, isn't the expectations from us high. It is for us to question ourselves whether we at all live up to the expectations of even being a human and to be called the most beautiful creation of Lord Almighty. It is really high time for all of us to think whether we have been born to work towards our self interests. Is it not being selfish? What is so great, if we spend years to earn handsome bank balance so that we can take care of our family members? Is it not our moral duty? Do not the animals also take care of their family members, the way we do? How then has our birth made a difference to this world?

If we leave this world without making a mark or impact, then would it have not been better that we had not born?

Look around the world and we will find so many like us craving for even the basic necessities of life; some for food, some for education, some others for shelter and what not. Today, they are on the receiving end, what if the tide changes and we end up in a similar situation. Who can say it will never happen to him? It would be foolish for someone to challenge something which is not in our control.

No one knows how much time is left for him. Do not waste it by creating something for your own interest rather invest your time in extending a helping hand to those who are in need. Live for others.

Selfless does not mean you do not earn or achieve something in life, what matters is the thought behind all these. If you wish to achieve something or earn heftily just because you want to be an inspiration to others or to contribute in others sustainability, then it is not being selfish.

Although it is for you to answer, I would wish to share this beautiful and meaningful line which I came across during my childhood - *Khud ke liye jiye toh kya khak jiye*... A life lived for one's selfish gains, is a life worth not lived.

DEEPIKA
FOUNDATION

This book supports "Deepika Foundation". As contribution to the society and humankind at large, 10% of the revenue generated through sales of this book will go as proceed to the foundation.

Deepika Foundation—*Bringing light to lives*